For Sofia, with love

Come on Arnie

Arnie is a little bird. He has got two brothers and two sisters. Their mother is bringing the food, because her children are very hungry. Hmmh, worms and bugs! One day mother says to the little birds: "Listen to me children, the day has come, you are old enough now. You must learn to fly!"

ARNE

His brothers and sisters try hard. Flying is not easy! But after a while they manage it and so they fly around, meet other birds and make new friends. "Do you want to come with us, Arnie?" they ask him. "Me? - Er, no!" Arnie says. "I'll stay here and relax a little bit. Have fun!"

Arnie eats the rest of the worms his mother has left and then sleeps a little bit. It's warm and cosy in the nest. Why leave it and fly around?

ARN

"Arnie, Arnie!"
Arnie looks up. His brothers and sisters have come home.
"Arnie, you won't believe what we saw! Wonderful trees and flowers, and lots of other birds!" they shout. "And now we are so hungry!"
And Arnie? Arnie is hungry, too. Of course.

On the next day his brothers and sisters ask him again: "Come on Arnie, don't you want to join us?" But Arnie doesn't want to. He can watch the sun, the trees and other birds from his nest. And his mum will bring him food. So everything is fine. Why learn to fly? He looks at the ground. Oh no, that's far too high! I could fall and hurt myself, Arnie thinks.

In the afternoon a storm suddenly comes. His family is out, Arnie is alone in the nest. The sky gets darker and darker and the wind begins to blow heavily. Arnie tries to hide, but he has no chance. The storm is too strong. So - oh no - he falls out of the nest!

Ouch, that hurts! Arnie gets up and looks around. He has never been anywhere else but in the nest. The trees seem to be very high. "Miaow, miaow!" What's that? Oh no! A cat! Arnie tries to run away but - he is too big to run. He can only walk very slowly. And flying? No chance! Arnie has never tried it before! And the cat is coming nearer and nearer! "Help!" Arnie cries.

ARNIE

Help, what's that? Suddenly Arnie is leaving the ground. Is he flying? No! An eagle is lifting him high up in the sky.
Puh, he is saved!

ARNIE

That wasn't funny!
Arnie is so scared. His heart is beating fast and he is shivering.
And now? He must sit here and wait for his mother and his brothers and sisters. And the silly cat is still there!
For the first time in his life Arnie thinks: I'm a bird and I'm far too fat to fly. That's not good! I must do something!

The next day, his brothers take Arnie to the flying school. He has some flying lessons there. At the beginning it's very hard. But Arnie gets better and better. And, what a surprise, flying is fun! Arnie plays with other birds in the forest. And he no longer eats so much. Look at him, he's fit now, isn't he?

Time for stories

Englische Lesehefte für die Klassen 3 bis 6

Paket 1 (je ein Exemplar Heft 1-5)

- Heft 1 Frosty the snowman
- Heft 2 Simon the sheep
- Heft 3 At the fair
- Heft 4 Happy Easter
- Heft 5 A really big fish

978-3-619-49150-6

Paket 2 (je ein Exemplar Heft 6-10)

- Heft 6 Come on Arnie
- Heft 7 Sea life
- Heft 8 Colourful world
- Heft 9 The little dragon
- Heft 10 What a night

978-3-619-49151-3

Die Hefte werden als Verpackungseinheit von 5 Stück geliefert.

9 783619 511600

Bestell-Nr. 5100-16
ISBN 978-3-619-51160-0